D0941312

Family Snaps™

Great Grandpa is WEIRD

Written by Stephanie Bilovsky
Illustrated by Tracy Bishop

Please visit our website at www.redchairpress.com.
Find a free catalog of all our high-quality products for young readers.

Great Grandpa is Weird!
Publisher's Cataloging-In-Publication Data
Bilovsky, Stephanie.
Great Grandpa is weird / written by Stephanie Bilovsky ; illustrated by Tracy Bishop.

pages : illustrations ; cm. -- (Family snaps ; [5])

Summary: To young boys and girls, the elderly can be full of mystery--sometimes seeming even weird and strange. When a young boy hesitates visiting his great grandpa, his mother's soothing words explain the love and the lifetime of memories our elders have to share with us.

Interest age level: 005-008.

ISBN: 978-1-63440-042-8 (library hardcover)

ISBN: 978-1-63440-043-5 (paperback)

Issued also as an ebook. (ISBN: 978-1-63440-044-2)

1. Grandparent and child--Juvenile fiction. 2. Reminiscing in old age--Juvenile fiction. 3. Families--Juvenile fiction. 4. Kindness--Juvenile fiction. 5. Grandparent and child--Fiction. 6. Reminiscing in old age--Fiction. 7. Families--Fiction. 8. Kindness--Fiction. I. Bishop, Tracy. II. Title. III. Series: Family snaps ; [5]

PZ7.1.B556 Gr 2016

[E] 2015938019

First published by:
Red Chair Press LLC PO Box 333 South Egremont, MA 01258-0333

Printed in the United States of America
Distributed in the U.S. by Lerner Publisher Services. www.lernerbooks.com

Uh-oh, I know where we're going. "Mama, no!"

"I'm not going in," I said as the car pulled up near the little house.

"But Baby," said Mama, "Poppy is my grandpa. That makes him your GREAT grandpa. That's very special."

“His voice is so scratchy. He sounds like a frog,” I groaned.

"One too many 'I love you's
talked his voice right out,"
said Mama.

"His hands are wrinkly like lizard claws,"
I pointed out.

"Sixty years in Grandma's hands have dried them out," smiled Mama.

“He can’t hear anything. It’s like talking to a fish,” I complained.

"Eighty years of stories have gone in those ears. It's hard to fit more in," said Mama.

“His mouth and face are so dry it scratches like a porcupine,” I whined.

"Hundreds of boo-boos have dried up the softness of his skin," said Mama.

“He just sits in that cold wheelchair,”
I said, “like a turtle stuck in his shell.”

“After thousands of walks, his feet got tired of stepping,” said Mama.

"He tells the same stories over and over," I said.

“That’s because he tells them once for you and again for all the angels listening in,” explained Mama.

“He stares at me funny, like a fly
who can’t tell what is real,” I said.

"Millions of memories dance in those eyes. Sometimes it's hard to know what is now and what is a memory," Mama said with tears in her eyes.

"Well, if he's all filled up with memories, why do we need to visit?" I asked.

Mama smiled, “So he can give some to us to carry.”

New memories are made every day.